The Lazy Lion

by June Woodman

Illustrated by Ken Morton

CHECKERBOARD PRESS

NEW YORK

It is the Jungle Sports Day.
The sun is hot and the path
is dusty. Lion is looking for
somewhere cool to rest.
"I need a good, long sleep,"
he says.
Soon he comes to the river
and stops for a drink.
Alligator is up a tree.
He is tying flags onto
a long string.

"Hey Lion! Can you help me?"
calls Alligator. Lion yawns.
"Not today. I am much too
tired," he says. "But why
are you tying flags, Alligator?"
he asks.
"Because . . . wo—o—o—o . . ."
Alligator trips over the
flags. SPLAT. He lands
in the mud.
"Never mind," says Lion, and
he goes on down the path.

He sees Kangaroo come bouncing
by with her baby in her pouch.
"Hello, Lion," shouts Kangaroo.
"Are you ready for the big day?"
"Not today, Kangaroo,"
says Lion. "I am much too
tired. What big day?" he asks.
"Sorry, Lion," says Kangaroo.
"Must be going. In training,"
and away she bounces.
"Never mind," says Lion.

Lion wanders on down the dusty path. Elephant is under the trees blowing up balloons.

"All these balloons," he says grumpily. "Will you hold some for me, Lion?"

"Not today," says Lion. "I am much too tired." Lion begins to walk away. He does not see the balloons lift Elephant off the ground.

Lion looks back. "Why are you blowing up balloons, Elephant?" he asks. But Elephant is not there. He is floating away above Lion's head.
"Never mind," says Lion.
He turns and walks on in search of a quiet place to sleep.

Lion sees Spider trying to put on his running shoes.
"Can you help me tie my shoes?" asks Spider. "I forget how to do it."
"Not today, Spider," says Lion. "I am much too tired. But why are you wearing running shoes?"
"I forget," says Spider, "but I know there is a good reason."
"Never mind," says Lion, as he walks on.

Parrot is trying to wind up
his stopwatch.
"Hello, Lion. Hello, Lion,"
says Parrot. "Can you help?
Can you help?"
"Not today. I am much
too tired," says Lion. "But
why are you winding up
a stopwatch?"
"Today is the day, today is
the day . . ." Parrot begins.
"Oh never mind," says Lion.

"That Parrot always says everything twice," says Lion as he gets back to his den. Ostrich is waiting for him. She has Lion's invitation to the sports day. "Hello, Lion," whispers Ostrich, starting to blush. She holds out the invitation.
"Not today, Ostrich," says Lion, "I am much too tired. What is it about, anyway?"

But Ostrich is so shy she puts
her bucket over her head
and she runs away.
"Never mind," says Lion.
He is too lazy to look at
the invitation.
"I think I will get a drink
before I settle down," he says
to himself. He wanders slowly
down to the river. Lion has
a drink and falls asleep.

He does not see that he is lying on the starting line. He does not notice the other animals lining up for the first race. He does not see Kangaroo bouncing up and down. Or Spider with his running shoes on. Or Hippo on tip-toes. Or Alligator tripping over his feet and falling into Ostrich.

He does not see Mouse standing
on a box, holding a starting
pistol. Or Parrot holding
the stopwatch.
Mouse calls out, "Ready,
Get Set . . ."
BANG! She fires the starting
pistol. Lion wakes up with
a start. He jumps to his feet
and runs off as fast as he can.

Lion runs past all the other animals. He runs through the finishing tape and keeps going until . . .BUMP! He crashes into Elephant. Elephant has just landed with his balloons. "Out of my way, Elephant!" shouts Lion. "Someone is shooting at me."

All the other animals come running up to Lion.

"Well done, Lion," they all shout. "You have won the race."

"In a world record. In a world record," says Parrot.

"Have a balloon," says Elephant.

"Not today, Elephant," replies Lion. "I am far too tired. I must find somewhere for a quiet sleep."

Here are some words in the story.

dusty   wearing

stops   twice

tying   waiting

training   blush

bounces   lazy

wanders   starting

quiet   past